D0996930

To my children, Courtney and Piers.
M. S.
For my sons, Philip, Gordon and Graham.
I. D.

First published in 1992
Text copyright © Michael Scott, 1992
Illustrations copyright © Ian Deuchar, 1992

Typeset by Deltatype Ltd, Ellesmere Port
Printed in Italy
for J. M. Dent & Sons Ltd
91 Clapham High Street
London SW4 7TA

British Library Cataloguing in Publication Data is available.

The illustrations for this book were prepared using
watercolour.

THE PIPER'S RING

Michael Scott
Illustrated by Ian Deuchar

Dent Children's Books · London

Sharp and clear on the cold morning air, the eagle heard the cry. It hovered on huge outstretched wings and tilted its head to one side, listening.

Below it the vast expanse of purple heather lay unbroken except for a single twisted tree in the middle of the heath. It heard the cry again. The eagle dropped, circling over the tree until it spotted a bundle tucked into the branches – it was a human child.

Long before the two figures came into sight, the eagle sensed the ancient magic surrounding them. The bird's wings snapped up, and it soared away, wondering what the Sidhe-folk could want with the child.

Moira was cold and wet. She had been standing in the river for more than an hour and had only caught one small fish. She wiped her bare feet on the grass and squeezed some of the water from the hem of her heavy skirt before climbing up onto the river-bank. She just had to feed the baby and then she could go on her way.

Moira made her way to the twisted tree. She stretched up to the branches where she had left her son – and gasped. There was no sign of the baby. Her heart pounded madly as she knelt on the soft ground beneath the tree and looked closely at the mud for any signs or tracks. There was nothing. Her son was gone.

Many hours later the villagers trudged wearily home. At the entrance to the village, where Moira and her father were standing, each one shook his or her head. They had searched for miles around, but they had not found the baby.

Moira buried her head in her hands and wept. Her father tried to comfort her.

He pointed to the cloudy sky where a faint line of silver showed on the horizon, "When the moon is full, we can go and visit the Wise Man. He will be able to help us."

The Wise Man sat in his cave before a huge fire. When Moira had finished her story he stretched out his hand until his fingertips touched the yellow and orange flames.

A picture appeared in the leaping flames: a flat heather-covered hillside, a single twisted tree, with a white cloth bundle high in the branches.

''My baby,'' Moira whispered.

Two figures appeared in the picture: tall, thin, sharp-faced women wrapped around in long shimmering robes. They stopped at the tree, reached up and took the baby.

The fire suddenly died.

''Your baby is gone,'' the Wise Man said sadly. ''The Sidhe have him, and whoever goes into the Sidhean does not return.''

''Help me – please,'' Moira begged.

The Wise Man sat back in the shadows. ''I cannot.''

''Then, who can?''

''The Piper!''

Moira stood on the hills overlooking the dark forest. Faint on the chill morning air, she heard the sound of pipes. She set off after the music.

The trees were old and twisted into strange and frightening shapes. Moss dripped from the curling branches and huge pale mushrooms grew in the places never touched by the sun. Moira hurried quickly down a thin winding path criss-crossed with animal tracks.

Suddenly the music stopped. Moira froze.

"Come forth," said a deep, strong voice.

As her eyes adjusted to the green gloom, she spotted a man almost invisible against the backdrop of the forest. He was dressed entirely in leaves of different trees, and his boots and belt had been made from bark. Perched on his knee was a long golden pipe.

"Come forth," the Piper said again, beckoning her. "I am the Piper. I know why you're here Moira."

"How do you know my name?" Moira gasped.

He smiled. "I am a half-Sidhe, my mother was human, my father was a lord amongst the Sidhe. He taught me their magic."

"Can you help me?" Moira asked softly.

"Tell me why I should help you," the Piper said.

"Because I love my son – he is all I have in this world."

"That's reason enough," the Piper nodded. "But there is one problem. I was allowed to return to the World of Men on condition that I never speak to any living person about the Sidhe . . ."

"But please, you must!"

The Piper leaned forward and placed a ring on her finger. "Sleep," he said quietly, "sleep and dream . . . and learn!"

Moira heard his voice echoing in her dream.

"The Sidhe folk need nothing, but want everything. They most desire the ancient magical treasures of this world. Offer them the Cloak of Nechtan and the Harp of Eisirt in return for your child."

"How shall I find these treasures?"

The Piper reached forward and touched the ring. "The answer is here on your finger. Go to the mouth of the largest cave you can find, call the Sidhe and name the treasures. They will come to you. Remember, if you are in danger, call upon the magic of the ring."

Moira awoke abruptly. She lifted her hand to look at the bone ring the Piper had given her. She saw a procession of tiny, delicate and beautiful figures carved into it: the skeleton of a whale, and a flight of countless seabirds. Moira had an idea.

It took her two days to reach the sea.

She walked the rocky beaches until she found the huge skeleton of a whale. Its bones were the purest white, polished by the weather. She picked the smallest, working them into the triangular shape of a harp, and then strung it with strands of moss and seaweed from the beach.

A dozen times she climbed the cliffs to steal tufts of down and feathers from the bird's nests. By the evening of the third day she had enough to begin to weave.

She worked tirelessly until she had made a fabulous cloak, woven from down and feathers and sewn together with strands from her own hair. She looped yellow seaweed in an intricate design around the edge of the cloak, and then fitted two white stones for the clasp.

The treasures were ready.

As the moon rose over the sea, Moira stood at the mouth of an enormous cave with the harp at her feet and the cloak over her arm.

"Sidhe . . . come forth!" she called, and the cave took her voice, making it echo, "Sidhe . . . Sidhe . . . Sidhesidhesidhe . . ."

Nothing happened.

Moira was about to call again when she suddenly smelt a strange bitter-sweet scent, like herbs or freshly cut grass. A tiny red light sparkled before her eyes – then yellow – then green.

Moira blinked her eyes hard as the piercing spots and twisting curls of colour danced before her.

When she opened them again, she was in the Sidhean.

The grass all around her was bright and green, the sky above her a perfect blue. Tiny brightly coloured flowers grew everywhere, but they were like no flowers she had ever seen, and the trees were slender and made of glass or metal, each one different: gold, silver and crystal.

The Fairy Host stood before her: tall and thin, pale-skinned, golden-haired, with high narrow cheekbones and slanting eyes. They wore shining, silken clothes, and jewellery of gold and crystal.

Two figures walked towards her. Moira knew immediately that they were the Sidhe king and queen. The queen was holding a small bundle in her arms.

"You are very brave," the king said quietly, his wide green eyes fixed on her face.

"Or very foolish," the queen added with a cold cruel smile. Her hair was the colour of old gold and fell to the ground behind her.

"I have come for my child," said Moira.

The queen hissed like a cat. "I shall never give him up."

Moira held up the two treasures. The king stepped forward.

"What have you got there?"

"The Cloak of Nechtan and the Harp of Eisirt."

The Sidhe Host murmured and whispered. The sound was like the wind rustling over a field of tall grass.

"Give them to me!" the king reached out a long-fingered, long-nailed hand.

"You may have the treasures in return for my son," Moira replied quietly.

"No," the queen snapped.

"Give her the babe," the king commanded. "These treasures are priceless. We can get another human child."

Moira thought the queen might refuse again, but suddenly she handed over the baby. The harp and cloak dropped to the ground as Moira took her son in her arms. With a cry of joy, she turned and walked quickly away from the Sidhe.

In front of her, through the doorway to her own world, she could see the moon shining high over a sparkling sea while all around her in the Sidhean it was daylight. She hurried on.

Behind her came a terrible cry of rage, and she heard the queen scream, "Tricked!"

Moira ran. She risked a single glance behind her . . . and saw the Sidhe knights, with swords drawn, galloping their wild-eyed horses towards her.

Moira clutched her son tightly to her and pulled the bone ring from her finger. She flung it towards the knights . . .

Instantly a forest of bones sprang up – tall bones, twisting yellow and white bones. Like the ribs of a great whale they formed a protective ring around her, keeping the Sidhe warriors away.

Then the birds appeared. They were tiny specks at first, like dust motes rising up from the ring. They grew and grew into a huge flock that flew at the fairy knights, pecking at them, cawing, flapping their wings, tearing with their claws and driving the knights back.

Moira threw back her head and laughed aloud as she ran out of the cave . . . and into the night.

She had saved her son from the Sidhe.

Moira's son grew up to be strong and handsome, with a great talent for music. His piping was so beautiful that people said it could even silence the birdsong.

But on certain nights, when the moon was full, he would walk the rocky beaches, playing his pipes . . . as if searching for something.

But even he did not know what he was looking for . . . and then the music of his pipes would sound like a child crying.